ISBN   978-0-9834831-4-4

Printed in the United States of America

Writing
an
Historical Novel

Warren Dent

Acknowledgments

I've read a lot of historical novels. I've even written a few. I've also read a lot of books of non-fictional history.

Which perhaps has spoiled me for reading historical novels.

For if the novels don't have their historical facts correct they lose their authenticity, and I find myself mentally correcting the errors and becoming distracted from what most likely is a good story.

So this is a thank-you to all those authors who spend time researching and checking the facts around historical events, and ancient cultural habits, practices, and beliefs.

Plus, it's a thank you to all those readers who enjoy how I integrate history into my stories. Culture is partially formed through new arrivals into an existing society telling of their experiences via stories. Story-telling is an art. Combining it with history is an undervalued capability.

Hopefully this little booklet will inspire more of you to do what I love doing – telling history through stories.

Dedication

To all those brave pioneers who gave up everything they treasured in their homelands and travelled to an unknown land and environment in order to provide a new life and better opportunities for their families and ensuing generations. We descendants should recognize their courage and commitment and record their stories for posterity.

Contents

1. **Introduction**

What has inspired you to think about writing an historical novel? Maybe you just read something about the Pharaohs of Egypt, or the First Nations people of Canada, or Captain Cooks' discovery of Australia. Or maybe you were recently chatting with Grandmother Maria who was telling tales about her grandma and grandpa when they migrated from Italy one hundred years ago. Or was it that movie you saw about the Civil War or the book you read about the Black Holocaust? Perhaps the more recent battle over the Falkland Islands, or a dream you had about ancient Greek Gods?

It really doesn't matter what has motivated you to think about writing. I can't remember what inspired me to first write an historical fiction story. I'm just glad I did it. Because it was a lot of fun, I learned a lot, and there are some readers out there who have come to enjoy what I was able to put together.

This little primer is aimed at helping you achieve similar results.

There are lots of famous authors who are recognized for their historical writings. Maybe you can become one of them. But even if you never achieve legendary recognition you can reap rewards from putting together your own work.   And today it's so much easier than it was even twenty years ago. Because of one huge change in all our lives – the presence and accessibility of the Internet.

But don't let me get ahead of myself here.   I'm going to start by assuming two things.

1. You have an historical period already in mind
2. You have some idea of a plot, characters, and events around which your story will revolve

It really is Ok if you don't have the second part fully hashed out in your mind. Sometimes inspiration comes as you research and dream, or as you put words to paper (so to speak). Don't feel ahead of time you must have everything 'buttoned up'. If you do, well and good. But many novels 'evolve' as you get to understand your characters more fully, as you get a systemic feel for the times you are writing about, and as your theme develops through unexpected associations and new opportunities.

But if you really don't have an historical period in mind, it might be helpful to look at some of the periods possible. There are hundreds literally, so if you've already chosen your period of interest you may want to skip this and the next paragraph. For those of you still reading here, let's make sure we understand what's meant by an historical novel. The Historical Novel Society's definition, for example, includes novels written at least fifty years after the events described, or novels written by people approaching the subject only via research. Clearly any of the following periods qualify: Prehistoric Times, Ancient History, Medieval, Renaissance, The Seventeenth Century, The Eighteenth Century, The American Old West, Nineteenth Century North America, Nineteenth Century Europe (includes the Napoleonic period), The Early Twentieth Century (1900-1919), The 1920s and 1930s and up to the 1950's, Pre-Columbian Times and the Spanish Conquest, Ancient, Golden Age and Pre-Colonial India, The Ottoman Empire, Colonial India.

Perhaps, however, you think by country or area. You can find areas of rich content in most places in the world, but here are some of the more popular: Egypt and the North, or South Africa, Elsewhere in Africa, China, Japan, Korea, Mongolia, Tibet, Nepal, Bhutan and Nomads of Eurasia, Southeast Asia, Australia, New Zealand, Post-Colonial India, Burma and Ceylon, The Caribbean, The Arabian Peninsula, Palestine, Israel, Syria, Lebanon, Turkey. Mesopotamia and Afghanistan, Persia. If you feel you don't know enough about these times or places, or you simply want to learn more about them, an excellent source of information is Margaret Donsbach's site http://www.historicalnovels.info/Best-Historical-Novels.html. Have a look at the links in the left hand sidebar.

Ok, so you have a period of history in mind. Good start. But what do you really know about it? Just what grandma told you, what you read in a specific book, or what you saw in a movie? Probably not enough frankly.

For an historical novel to be acceptable, at a minimum it must be credible with respect to the facts of the times. They certainly didn't have showers as we know them in ancient Egypt, and the first steam engine tramway locomotive appeared in Wales in 1804, not earlier anywhere else. Things you might assume have been around forever probably haven't. Kids' strollers turned up first in the late 1840s. Before that babies were pushed around in 'perambulators' or 'prams'. One even has to be careful with common phrases. If you want to talk about a couple in the 19th Century, you'd better not have them refer to the notion that 'it takes two to tango' since the Tango dance wasn't invented until 1912.

As Margaret Donsbach says: 'You do have to get the customs and technological details right. Did people use forks yet while dining? What type of head covering would your heroine have worn?'

Details like this can be maddening to research, because most historians focus on political structures and on changing religious and philosophical beliefs. The Historical Novelists Center has articles and bibliographies of sources that offer a starting point in researching for the type of information that historical novelists such as you and I need in order to place our characters in an authentic day-to-day physical setting.

But, as I mentioned above, there's a great tool available to help – The Internet. One has to thank many research institutions, historical societies, governments, certain private companies, and Wikipedia for their support in making old data and information available on the Internet. And new data is constantly being added, so if you don't find what you want immediately, just wait a little.

A great example of this notion is a story from February 2012 about the discovery of the history of more than three thousand slaves in Virginia, USA over three and a half centuries before. The following link http://www.cnn.com/2012/02/05/us/virginia-slaves/index.html?hpt=hp_t3 carries a story of how a historical society in Virginia, where slavery began in the American colonies in 1619, discovered the identities of 3,200 slaves from unpublished private documents which provide new information for today's descendants in a first-of-its-kind online database. Many of the slaves had been forgotten to the world until the Virginia Historical Society received a $100,000 grant to pore over some of its eight million unpublished manuscripts. Letters, diaries, ledgers, books and farm documents from Virginians dating back to the 1600s revealed information about the long-lost identities of the slaves. The private nonprofit historical society, the fourth-oldest in the nation, is assembling a growing roster of slaves' names and other information, such as the slaves' occupations, locations and plantation owners' names. The free, public website also provides a high-resolution copy of the antique documents that identify each slave.

Hopefully you won't have to wait nearly four hundred years for the information you want, but remind yourself to constantly check for changes on our electronic information highway, the Internet. New sources literally emerge hourly.

2. *The Characters, Plot, and Setting*

So now you know in what time period and place your novel will take place. Good. And you have an idea of the story you want to tell. You have a list of the main characters, either on paper, or in your head.

Quick, if they are in your head, put them on paper, now! And while you are about it, start setting out some sort of diagram or table that shows the years your story covers. That's not a bad idea even if all your action takes place within the same year or even the same month.

One suggestion; if this is a story about your own family think well about whether you want to publish to the world the historical antics of your ancestors. They may reflect on you. Especially if a good part of your story is fiction that you make up. Will your highly voluble cousin get irritated at what you say about her? Will your brother argue about your interpretation of the reason your parents moved from the country to the city? And do you really think you know your grandparents interests better than everyone else?

And here's a very simple trick. If you are going to write about your ancestors, write your novel using all your family names. It will be far easier than if you start with fake names to disguise your family. Then if you use Microsoft Word, you can use the autocorrect process to replace your family name 'Wright' with 'Williams' or whatever you choose, in order to effect the disguise. As soon as you type the word 'Wright' it will magically transform to 'Williams' and you won't lose a beat in the train of thought you are describing.

Or you can do this when finished with the 'Replace' command applied throughout your document.

Now, have you chosen names for your characters already (family or otherwise)? Have you checked that those names were in vogue in the period you are writing about? The name Anne-Marie, as much as you think it is pretty, wasn't around in the 1860s when civil war broke out. Try a search on 'Civil War female names'.

Not only do you have to give your characters relevant names, you must dress them appropriately too. You'd lose credibility with women wearing bras in the mid-19th century as the first 'breast supporter' was patented in 1893. You could do a little better with swimsuits, as by 1855 they were well in vogue. Women wore bonnets in Victorian and earlier times, and men have worn hats since ancient Greek times.

But your plot can't have folks riding bicycles much before 1865. People walked to visit neighbors in nearby villages, and children literally did walk miles to school if they lived on farms. For long distance visits people bought tickets for train rides. But not before 1800. Hospitals for treatment of disease and suffering have been around since medieval times, but they weren't always close by.

So make sure your plot doesn't make assumptions that just weren't appropriate in your time of record. And remember, communication was by word of mouth and the reading of paper scrolls for years before the telegraph and phone were invented.

One thing you have going for you perhaps is that crime seems to have been around since man turned up on this planet. Prostitution, robbery, torture, and murder have been written about for centuries. As have nuns, priests, artists, bureaucrats, farmers and royalty. Hunting, and the cultivating of crops and other foods has always existed to provide sustenance for man. Animals often lived with people or were in herds they managed for furs or meat. Hygiene and sanitation are modern words.

Speaking of food, remember in 'olden' times there was a lot less processed food available. No McDonalds either. People bought fresh produce often daily at the local market. Why? No iceboxes or refrigerators before 1830s. Farmers were well regarded, as they grew the produce that sustained the town folk and brought it to market making it easy for them to buy.

And of course the common folk didn't have fine bone china dinner plates and nice silver knives and forks. For pioneers, the dining table was crudely hand made. Wardrobes, and kitchen cupboards were made by village craftsmen.   Beds were sometimes just mattresses on the floor, or on cast iron frames. Make sure your assumptions about furniture fit the period. Some of it was absolutely beautiful of course. It's possible that your story even centers about a piece that had been handed down in your family over generations. If only it could tell a story about all it had seen over the years.

Also, remember indoor plumbing was a treat when it finally arrived. Those outdoor 'privies' weren't real pleasant. What some of our ancestors put up with would shock us if we had to take their place.

Speaking of which, some of your best inspiration could well come from your family.   Did grandma hum a tune from the old land when she rocked you as a baby? Have you asked her about it? Are there any old bibles at home which have been in the family for years and that have names inscribed in the inside cover? Does grandpa have a series of ancient sepia photographs in the tin where his old smelly pipe still lies? Is there a dried flower between the pages of a book that Aunt Susan said she read as a youngster? Look around. You may be surprised at what you can find that gives you another thought, or another insight into your story. And don't be reticent to ask. Older folks generally love telling how life was different in their days. What the school-house and school-marm were like and how much a bottle of milk cost.

Speaking of the school house reminds me of another technique – the third party approach. Maybe grandma today can't really get through to granddaughter Sally about sailing ships crossing the oceans in years gone by. But describing a sea voyage could be enhanced by using a teacher to show children the route on a globe. Also, one could use the sweet innocence of young children to ask questions that might be hard to ask otherwise. "Why did grandpa board the ship, but grandma didn't?"

A teacher can also introduce pictures and/or descriptions of objects/events/activities that can become the basis of knowledge for inquiries from unrelated sources beyond those the mainstream characters have access to. Angela and her mother Amanda had traveled to the old country to meet Angela's dying grandmother Fabiola. "Would you like a piece of fruit?" Fabiola asked Angela, holding out a small wicker basket filled to the brim. "What kind of fruit is that?' interrupted Amanda. "Mom, these are figs. We learnt all about how they are grown in class."

3. **Timing within the story**

Whether you are dealing with one month in the life of some specific character, or one year, or decades, or generations, you could probably find it useful to set out a visual chart of your period on a piece of paper beside you. We mentioned this above. Sometimes when the creative streak hits and words just flow like there was no tomorrow you may not remember when those two sons got married, or exactly when Uncle Henry died. But readers will spot incongruities and mistakes very readily. They've become wrapped in your story and are living the life you've so vividly portrayed of dear old Sam. And woe betides you if you forget when his mistress gave birth to his first illegitimate child, or you make the child seem older than she really is at some point through the actions you ascribe to her.

Just as you will spend time really getting to develop your characters, make sure you are just as aware of what time of year it is when events take place. In most places roses bloom in summer, so don't have a maiden gently holding one to her chin in the garden in winter. Don't pick apples or vegetables out of season, and don't have trees generating new leaves in autumn.

Sometimes in fact you may add an event that you had never originally planned. Inspiration came out of the blue and you thought of something meaningful to include. It's possible that it is so significant that you have to adjust all the previous dates. Having a record of what happened when, will allow you to preserve events in sequence and timing when you have to make those inevitable adjustments.

And if writing within a microcosm of time, make sure you leave enough time to get from place A to place B. Walking takes longer than riding in a carriage behind a horse, which takes longer than riding the horse per se, which takes longer than traveling in a car, or bus, or train in most cases. And ships transporting individuals across the seas can take ages, and are often beset by storms or other unnatural events. Remember the Titanic?

One of the fun things to write about if one has a novel which extends through five decades or more is how things change - inventions of new tools, new architectural designs, discoveries of passages and routes, industrial processes, machinery of war, or technology in the broadest sense. Things we take for granted today can be big surprises in earlier times. Even in nature – look at how the discovery of the platypus caused consternation in scientific circles back in London – was this real or a hoax? If your story includes orchids or roses, new varieties are announced every year. Is there someone with a green thumb in your story?

What do we marvel at today? The Concorde which flew at 60,000 feet at twice the speed of sound? Trains in Japan and France that can travel at 250 mph or more? Rockets carrying everyday billionaire citizens into space? Phones that are cameras and video players? Cars that run purely on batteries? One risk in writing is to sit back in time and project the then-future based as you know it today. One hundred, even fifty years ago, regular citizens couldn't conceive of the items listed above. Be careful to not stretch even what folks could dream about based on today's know-how and capabilities.

Sometimes we look back and marvel at what folks put up with in olden times. We despair at how hard their lot was, and this influences the subtle messages we unwittingly incorporate into our story. But while technology over time has lightened many of our loads, one cannot project that in time past everyone was unhappy with their burdens in life. In most cases they knew no better as they weren't aware of alternatives. And remember they were usually better off than their parents. In some cases that was reward enough.

The message here is that when writing about the past it's important to lay aside what one knows of today. One must get well and truly into the period of the story, and into the heads and habits of your characters. Read books from or about the period, but remember even those may not give truly accurate portrayals but just how an author thought about things. One needs to find common themes or descriptions across several books before locking into the assumption that your notions are really valid.

To reiterate something said before – the Internet is an incredible font of information. But some of that information is inaccurate or true dis-information. Anyone can get access to the Internet today and can put their thoughts out in blog form for the world to discover. Rants, raves, and rumors, along with blatant lies and threats can be made public as easily as true information and knowledge can be disseminated. Don't just rely on a single source, but check several to see if a common theme or incident or cause or philosophy is expounded in slightly different ways. Only then should you feel more comfortable. And if it sounds too good to be true, it probably isn't true. The Internet generates 'urban legends' as quickly as they can be written. And it is sad that so many folk are gullible enough to perpetuate them. If ever in doubt check www.snopes.com which is one great source for dispelling modern myths about the present and the past.

An example will illustrate. If your hero or heroine is an outdoors person in a climate with low outdoor temperatures at times, you may have him or her always wearing a cap or hat because of the belief that '75 percent of body heat is lost through the head alone'. Today we know that's a myth (there are many sources on the topic similar to http://voices.yahoo.com/heat-loss-through-head-fact-fiction-6843360.html), but if your story occurs before 1950 or even 1970 then using that belief would be Ok as no-one had public evidence to the contrary at those times. Even after those dates the myth was not undone until after 2007.

The moral? Check every assumption you make.

4. *Detail*

How much detail do you include, how much do you exclude? There's a thin dividing line here and various opinions and revealed behaviors can be found wherever you read about historical novels. There are those like Persia Woolley who will say that readers want to read about people and not about facts, so don't load down your narrative with stuff that doesn't impact the plot or the characters -- instead, you might follow Carson McCullough's example and save that info for a glossary in the back of your book.

There's no question that readers want to hear about other humans' foibles. But I really don't see relegating detail to a glossary. People want to know information as revealed in the flow of the story, not have to stop and check a glossary and then try to remember exactly the point being made when they return to the tale. And dare I suggest that one of the more potentially interesting and rewarding tenets of an historic novel is to actually educate the audience of readers. I can't imagine reading an historical novel where I didn't learn something new. Even Agatha Christie threw new ideas and facts at us through her variety of characters, albeit in multiple tales set in the identical time period. The question is where to draw the line between too little and too much detail. My suggestion is to err on providing more rather than less.

Why?

Another example. Ken Follett in 'Pillars of the Earth' is an obvious student of Middle Ages church architecture. He's done an incredible amount of research, and provides design conundrums and construction techniques that his builders must solve.   For me, by the time he has someone building church number four, I've had enough detail and so I skim-read through that section, slowing down when the main theme is once again being developed.   Maybe an arts or architecture aficionado would love hashing through how the spiral stairs are built or how the bell-tower is shaped but once I've learned that the character in question has remarkable skills in design and construction I don't need a lot more.

Leaving out detail can make it awkward for readers to always gauge context.   And while it's fair (and possibly even captivating) to leave certain details to the reader's imagination, in new environments one needs to provide plenty of context so the reader isn't left confused or feeling inadequate at not understanding a particular situation or action.

With respect to the notion of providing education for a reader, there are direct and indirect ways to do that.   The direct way is to show how a specific character thinks or acts, as in Ken Follett's novels.   But one can also make information flow indirectly.   For example you can have visitors or relatives talk about something new they've observed.   Or you can have a character read a book or newspaper that reveals information about a special topic.

Intermingling educational detail, beyond pure situational detail, richens a tale in my view.   The reader is getting 'something for nothing' in a way.   So think about adding information by weaving it into the relevant situation and making it integral to the story.   Sometimes easier said than done I'll admit, and you may have to make several tries via varied drafts before you feel comfortable.   My notion – if the judgment line is thin – is to go a little over the line rather than stop before it.   But be sensitive to context.

If it's a very special dinner you are writing about, then detailing the crochet work in the tablecloth may well be appropriate.   But if it's just the family discussing the latest village gossip over the evening meal I wouldn't bother.   Another technique to add detail that sometimes helps with its uniqueness is in flashback or 'recollection' scenes.   As Mary is talking to her best friend Jane she can say 'did I tell you that mother and I went to the opera in its new home last week? The building is ultra-modern with high-vaulted ceilings that enhance the sound, plus more comfortable, staggered seats that offer greater leg room and better sighting of the stage. (Elaborate as necessary…). We had a wonderful evening.'

Even with the best of intentions one can certainly overdo it. Ken Follett's 'Fall of Giants' goes into almost step by step description of battles within World War 1.   Incredibly boring unless you are a war buff. The mud on soldiers' boots became mud in my eye since it was described so often.   And the characters of the 'Giants' were over-shadowed by far too much detail on dressing, mannerisms, and other miscellaneous descriptions.

An interesting observation is that in my experience, readers of historical novels in particular seem to love wanting to learn how homes in earlier times were built, organized, decorated, and managed, and how folks lived in them. Perhaps in our busy, machine processed world of today we like to read about simpler ideals, hand-made items and artifacts, and the dying art of human craftsmanship. Or maybe we like to read about what seem to be primitive arrangements in order to contrast them with the luxuries we enjoy today. But great grandma crocheting doilies, great grandpa carving a flute, dried flowers as wall decorations, a clothes wringer on top of the washing cauldron, or bread deliveries by horse and cart, create images that usually elicit a wry, happy smile as they trigger a reader's memory.

You probably already know that you must employ an editor to read your work, but even as you proceed don't hesitate to get some objective friend to read over sections of your work to get honest off-the cuff independent feedback. Does it seem confusing? Is there too much detail or not enough explained? Do the characters seem too unreal? Are you using modern idioms which may not have applied in the time of the story? Is the story believable, etc.? You can ignore feedback if it's negative, or do what the toothpaste advertisers do which is solicit more opinions until you finally get to four out of five who like your work,. Preferably you will take the input to heart and adjust your story appropriately.

Of course there's another form of detail for which similar warnings apply although the reasons are different. I refer to graphical detail associated with acts on and between humans. Some authors love describing gore, especially in war scenes. Some readers love reading about gore because they probably will never experience it first hand, and their senses can be titillated appropriately. Just as there's an audience for horror movies and horror stories so is there a desire in many readers to be taken out of their comfort zones and to read about activities they themselves could never experience or even describe. Not just war but murders, especially stabbings it seems, give authors great license to describe agony and body parts in detail. Do your readers need that over and over? Maybe once would be enough? I've always wondered why Ken Follett felt compelled to repeatedly describe innards exposed after sword cuts to bellies.

And there are two other aspects that are relevant here. One is medicine. Bloodletting in the Middle Ages is one thing, surgeons operating even fifty years ago (that's 1963 for those mathematically challenged) used invasive techniques that can be described in wonderfully lurid detail if you so desire. Does it register in your memory that Dr. Christiaan Barnard performed the first human heart transplant in 1967? (So none before then please in your story).

And finally there's sex. Oh yes, it's a part of everyday life, so everyone is aware of it. Everyone. An important part of life actually. After all, intercourse is how you and I got here in the first place. (I know there are exceptions). It's been around since man and woman first played together. And it won't go away soon. The question is just how graphic do you want your descriptions to be? If you are squeamish about going into detail, that question is resolved. If not you probably have to think about how relevant a more graphic description might be. Could be very fitting in certain circumstances. In Jean Auel's magical series on prehistoric man there were times when sex detail was very appropriate. Yet she always offered it in good taste.

As writers we're also conscious that 'sex sells'. Look at how magazines and newspapers have degenerated to include semi-naked female image offerings purely for prurient attraction. In 'World Without End' Ken Follett breaks up the story regularly with sexual episodes that could just as easily be left out.

Only you can decide how much detail to include. If it's not germane to the story you might want to minimize it, but even so if you think it will help readers buy and read, then add it in. There's no requirement that a reader absorb every word you write. Just as one can mute the TV one can skip reading paragraphs in a book.

5. *Still Committed?*

Good. But in case you are getting just a little bit jaded and unsure about things, let me present some inputs that might help. Take a break for a minute and see if there's something below that inspires.

Peter Damien Ryan:
"We can become intrigued by romance, unfettered ambition, murderous intrigue, political manipulations, unbridled passions - and the humanity of the people who strode across history's stage so much larger than life."
(http://ezinearticles.com/?10-Best-Historical-Novels&id=5557006)

Margaret Donsbach:
"My favorite historical novels have characters that pull me right inside their skin so I can see (and hear, and smell) their time and place through their perspective. The lovely, clean prose either disappears into the world of the story, or it sings to me and carries me along without a misplaced bump or squeal. The best novels also give me something worthwhile to think about: a haunting idea, a new way of seeing something, or a question about human nature to ponder long after I've turned the last page. They never, ever bore me. My favorite novels straddle the boundary between literary and popular fiction, giving me rich characters and ideas along with a lively story with twists and turns that keep me wondering what will happen next."
(http://www.historicalnovels.info/Best-Historical-Novels.html)

Andrew Miller:

"... for others – and there are many of us – history was always a rattle-bag of wonderful stories. As a boy I understood perfectly that history is not something apart from us, sealed off. It is in our blood, our music, our language, the buildings we pass on the way to work. And at its best, historical fiction is never a turning away from the Now but one of the ways in which our experience of the contemporary is revived."
(http://www.guardian.co.uk/books/2011/jun/29/andrew-miller-top-10-historical-novels)

And a couple of other explanatory rather than inspirational remarks by authors I've referred to above.

Ken Follett:

"I like to create imaginary characters and events around a real historical situation. I want readers to feel: OK, this probably didn't happen, but it might have."
(http://www.brainyquote.com/quotes/keywords/historical_2.html#ixzz1n5Jn59bW)

Jean M. Auel

"Though my books are written from a historical perspective, I have gone so far back that I am in the realm of prehistorical speculation rather than simple historical fact to weave my stories around. "
(http://www.brainyquote.com/quotes/keywords/historical_9.html#ixzz1n5MXUH7V)

6. *What's next?*

There are lots of other things to talk about – such as resources that may be helpful, the art of writing and story-telling, and publishing. On writing, it's valuable to read others' suggestions, but in the end it's your story. You have to make sure you get your story told with the significance of individual points brought out as you want them.

You might think about the goals you have for writing this novel. Is it mainly for your own benefit to record ideas and thoughts in a different time dimension? Is it a family history, fictionalized, to be left as a legacy for your children and their children? Or is it to be a blockbuster novel that millions will want to read?

I'm not going to tell you how to discipline yourself to the process of writing – you have to set your own rules, procedures, timetable and motivation. But the goals you have may well impact how you go about recording your creativity and the time you allocate to so doing.

Here are some references that can help you with the writing process. They are general in nature, not necessarily specific to historical novel writing. They are taken from http://www.historicalnovels.info/Writing-Historical-Fiction.html

An article in the 2011 New Yorker: Therapist for Blocked Writers.

"Plot" by Ansen Dibell

"The First Five Pages "by Noah Lukeman (2000).

"The Plot Thicken"s by Noah Lukeman (2002).

"Writing the Breakout Novel" by Donald Maass.

But now for some references directed specifically at historical novel writing.

James Thom in http://www.historicalnovels.info/Art-and-Craft-of-Writing-Historical-Fiction.html warns about believing everything you can read on the Internet and urges lots of research. (We speak the same language clearly). Which reminds me. Research takes time, so stop thinking now that you are going to complete your novel in three months because you already know so much.

Elizabeth Crook includes an excellent article on her website about the "Seven Rules for Writing Historical Fiction". Here they are summarized

Rule #1: Sweat the Small Stuff-> Check your assumptions, add detail
Rule #2: Dump the Ballast -> Don't over-detail, make sure the story flows
Rule # 3: Keep Your Conscience Clean -> Make sure you know 'why' something was done
Rule #4: Resist Judging Your Characters -> In times past, values were different
Rule #5: Watch Out for First Person -> Can be a trap for over-indulging oneself
Rule #6: Don't Get Bogged Down by Back-story -> Let it come through gradually
Rule #7: Anticipate a Long Process -> With proper research may take a year

"How to Write and Sell Historical Fiction" by Persia Woolley (1997)

"Writing Historical Fiction" by Marina Oliver (2005).

7. *Finally - publishing*

Even if you think your novel-in-progress might have what it takes to hit the bestseller list, be prepared to work hard to make money. First you have to find an agent who can help you. You can search on the Internet for 'publishing agent' and find lots of sources. Here's one that seems to offer a straightforward process, is free, and has been recognized seven years in a row as one of the best websites for writers http://www.agentquery.com/. Getting rich from writing however is a goal not easily achieved. You may want to read http://www.genreality.net/the-reality-of-a-times-bestseller where Lynn Viehl who had a bestseller in July 2008, shares the nitty-gritty details of best-seller finances.

An option is to self-publish or to use POD ("print-on-demand") publishers. There are an increasing number available today. The simplest and probably least expensive is CreateSpace (www.creeatespace.com), an affiliate of Amazon.com, but as with all POD publishers the marketing of your book will be totally up to you. Pricing varies with POD publishers. Some charge an upfront fee and guarantee minimal distribution. You can pay extra for design and consultant services. Essentially, for any story of length your book will be printed only in black and white – color is very expensive and tends to be reserved for short books (less than 30 pages – such as children's tales). If you have diagrams or images to include you will have to be patient and make sure they are of high resolution (at least 300 dpi) and that the exact size is used in your word document, or the resolution will be reduced. As well, most publishers will want you to have written permission to use images you derive from other sources.

Make sure you read the publisher's contract to see what ownership rights you have and what information you must provide. Once again your royalty will seem quite low relative to the price someone pays for your book, so be prepared. As a last check you might like to read http://www.writershelper.com/self-publishing.html and http://www.sfwa.org/for-authors/writer-beware/pod/ which both discuss the pros and cons of self-publishing.

8. *Go for it!*

Congratulations! If you've made it this far you've kept up your enthusiasm despite some of the caveats and realism I've thrown your way. Good for you!   If you have a desire to pen a story that occupies a time over fifty years ago, go for it!, Writing can not only be a lot of fun, but incredibly rewarding as well. I have no doubt you will learn much as you conduct research on the things you think are relevant and that you will even find some information you hadn't thought about but which you can incorporate into your story. And you will feel good to have put something together that's been lingering in your mind or heart.

If you haven't done much writing before you may find the discipline of typing out your story a bit of a challenge. There are no rules – some folks can sit and write without notes and can type for hours on end. Some have to have the themes for each chapter written on a 3" x 5" card and take a week to write a chapter of just a few pages. Sometimes joining a writing club or a class on blogging will give you inspiration as you hear that there are other folks just like you.

But please, whatever you do, don't hesitate. Start writing today. Now. As you finish reading this. Even if you only jot notes about a new thought, or something you must mention in your book, or the title, or an outline, or an image or place you must describe. Remember 'DO' is halfway to being 'DONE'. Start now, and good luck!

About the Author

Warren Dent was born in Sydney, Australia. After gaining degrees in Canberra and Adelaide and a Ph.D. at the University of Minnesota, he taught Econometrics and Business Statistics for many years, before entering the private sector, where he worked for three number one companies – Eli Lilly, American Airlines, and Microsoft - creating new businesses and applying information systems to strategic market applications. Married, with four grown daughters, he now lives with his wife Gail in Seattle. Personal interests include boating and tennis. With numerous academic publications to his credit, and hundreds of business presentations behind him, he has recently turned his writing talents to more personal endeavours. Short story mysteries and longer historical fiction novels are his primary interests. Warren is a member of the Association of Personal Historians, ghost writing personal family histories and memoirs. His website is www.krandis.com, his email address is warren@krandis.com and his books may be found at http://www.amazon.com/-/e/B00744PW8U .

www.ingramcontent.com/pod-product-compliance
Lightning Source LLC
Chambersburg PA
CBHW071318200626
46813CB00015B/2258